Enjoy!
Jonk
x

In this story ...

CW00867560

SUGAR - Hannah's toy fair
changes colour, her mag
can make you grow (or shrink) and
she sings ALL THE TIME!

BLAZE - My toy dragon. He snorts
fire and he can fly, but he is
a bit scared of pretty much
everything.

HANNAH - I've tried to draw her name to show you what
she's like. She jumps into things and has lots of feelings
and stuff.

JO - That's me! I'm just me really. But every time we have a
magical adventure with Sugar and Blaze, I'm the one who
writes it down.

THIS is our latest adventure...

The Sugar and Blaze Adventures
Have you read them all?

That's Rubbish! ☐

Tinselpants! ☐

Prince Charm-Bin! ☐

Nuts! ☐

NUTS!

Jenny York

ILLUSTRATED BY LUKE COLLINS

For all you aunties out there.

You are awesome! x

Find out more about Jeny York by visiting www.jennyyork.com

First published in Great Britain in 2021 by Saltaire Books, Bradford, England.

CHAPTER ONE

It was the weekend before BONFIRE NIGHT!

Are you a Bonfire Night fan? Or do you prefer Halloween?

For me, Bonfire Night is the clear winner. You see, on the weekend closest to Bonfire Night me and my little sister Hannah go to stay with our aunties.

Just us. No parents!

It's kind of a tradition in our family now. We eat toffee apples and carve pumpkins. Dad says our aunties spoil us rotten and to be honest, they do.

It's awesome!

So...apart from the spoiling us rotten thing what can I tell you about my aunties?

Well, my Aunt Nina is the sensible one. She's thoughtful and kind and she loves to cook.

And then there's Aunt Zee - the bonkers one! She likes to be silly all the time.

Anyway, to understand how our autumn adventure started, I need to tell you about the pumpkins.

It was Friday teatime and we were sitting with our aunties in their kitchen carving pumpkins...

"I think you've made its mouth a bit too big!" worried Aunt Nina as she looked at Aunt Zee's pumpkin.

"I meant to make it that big!" said Aunt Zee. **"Because he's yawning!"**

Hannah giggled.

"He was up VERY late last night at a party," Aunt Zee explained, **"dancing the night away. He's a great dancer. Look!"**

Aunt Zee picked up her yawning pumpkin and began springing and spinning around the kitchen with it.

"See!" she cried. **"Great dancer!"**

But then she tried to do the splits and tripped over a chair with a clatter.

"He's okay!" she shouted, waving the pumpkin above her head. **"He's still dancing!"**

Hannah and I were laughing our heads off by this point and even Aunt Nina half smiled as she sighed and shook her head.

"Yours looks great, Jo!" said Hannah, as we

all went back to our carving. "Is that Blaze?"

"Well, it's supposed to be," I grinned.

Instead of cutting the usual scary face, I'd carved out the silhouette of my toy dragon, Blaze.

Now you might think that I'm a bit too old for a fluffy blue dragon toy, but there's something you should know!

Blaze was a gift from my Grandma and at the same time Hannah got this toy fairy, Sugar.

Sounds normal so far, right?

WRONG!

Because no one else knows but these two toys come to life!

Sugar becomes a colour-changing, constantly-singing nightmare that my sister adores...

4

and Blaze becomes a real dragon that can fly and breathe fire!

Even better, with the help of Sugar's magical dust, Blaze can grow as big a car.

And having a massive flying dragon that breathes fire comes in handy more often than you'd think...

Because since we got the toys, me and Hannah sort of **stir up** magical trouble.

Anyway, back to the story...

Once we'd finished carving, we took the pumpkins out into the front garden. Then we balanced them on the wall near the drive so that people walking past would see them.

Aunt Nina lit the candles and we all stood back to admire our hard work.

"I'm going to call my pumpkin **Nutzo!**" said Zee, her eyes twinkling. "Because of the O-shaped mouth and because pumpkins are my favourite autumn nut!"

"Pumpkins are **not** a type of nut!" laughed Aunt Nina. "The only nut around here is you!"

"I really like the o-shaped mouth though!" said Hannah kindly. "It makes him look like he's singing!"

"**Exactly!**" smiled Zee, shifting her pumpkin to the front. **"Nutzo's gonna be a pop star!"**

"I thought he was a dancer," said Aunt Nina moving Nutzo back into line with the others.

"Both" grinned Zee, lifting it forward again, **"A famous pumpkin popstar AND a dancer...and a decoration. Oh he's soooooo talented!"**

Just then, a tiny movement caught my eye near the bushes. A streak of black. As if the shadows had become an animal. As if the darkness itself had swirled into a living thing and then DARTED AWAY.

I squinted around the garden...but nothing moved again.

"What's up?" said Hannah, touching my arm.

I turned back to face her and as I did, the pumpkin candles flickered. For a split second, Nutzo looked different. Almost like he was screaming!

And then, a real SCREAM screeched out through the night!

AAAAAAAAAAAAAAAARRRRRRRRR

CHAPTER TWO

"Don't panic!" grinned Aunt Zee. **"That's just our neighbour, Mrs Poshpants!"**

Hannah snorted a giggle and Aunt Nina pursed her lips.

"Zee, you know very well that her name is **Mrs Possant,"** she hissed, **"NOT Mrs Poshpants!"**

"Oh, I'm rubbish with names!" shrugged Zee, giving me a secret wink and whispering, "she's super posh! Come on! I'll show you!"

We squelched over the muddy lawn towards

the low bushes that separated the two front gardens.

Mrs Poshpants was standing next to a man with lots of boxes who I guessed must be Mr Poshpants.

Everything next door, including Mr and Mrs Poshpants themselves, looked expensive and a bit too perfect to be friendly, if you know what I mean?

And right at that moment Mrs Poshpants might have had perfect make up, but her actual face was bright red! Like a balloon that might burst at any second!

"CAT POOP AGAIN!" she shrieked, hopping about as she tried to check the bottom of her shoes. "It's...I've...argghhhh!"

She stumbled into Mr Poshpants, who dropped his boxes with a

CRASH!

"Erm, everything OK over there?" called out Aunt Nina.

In a flash, the couple scrambled to put on a

show of being perfect.

"Fine! Fine!" waved Mr Poshpants and he pointed to the boxes on the ground as if he'd put them there on purpose. "Just been to get some fireworks for Bonfire Night."

"We got the most expensive ones they had," boasted Mrs Poshpants, looking smug. "Nice to celebrate, isn't it?"

"And here's an interesting fact for you..." called Mr Poshpants, not waiting for an answer. "...Did you know that fireworks were first made in China? **Course you didn't!** Me and my interesting facts, eh?"

"Smarty-bum," muttered Aunt Zee under her breath.

"What's that?" he called, raising an eyebrow.

"She said **'Lots of fun!'**" yelled Aunt Nina quickly, giving him a double thumbs up.

"Right you are!" he nodded. "Well, I'm off inside to do my sudoku. That's a sort of puzzle, you know. You really should try it. They do make easy ones for people like yourself."

Aunt Zee looked cross at this but Aunt Nina put a hand on her arm in a 'leave it' sort of way.

Mr Poshpants headed off, but Mrs Poshpants came towards us, peering suspiciously into our front garden.

"I really must give you the number for our gardener," she said, looking disapprovingly at the grass on our side.

"Erm…yeah, thanks." said Aunt Nina, frowning slightly. "Well, if you're sure you're alright…?"

Aunt Nina started turning to leave but this seemed to be the question Mrs Poshpants had been waiting for.

"It's that **dreadful cat** from number 26!" she hissed, looking desperate. "I mean you **know** how I love a neat garden. Says a lot about a person, a nice, tidy garden…"

Aunt Nina gave the wild jungle on our side of the bushes an uneasy glance but nodded.

"…But that **beast of a thing,"** growled Mrs Poshpants, "keeps leaving me **little** presents everywhere!"

"Presents!" gasped Aunt Zee and her eyes sparkled with mischief. "How lovely! What sort of presents? Personally, **I love a good necklace!"**

"No!" said Mrs Poshpants, looking suddenly uncomfortable. "Not actual presents. I mean..."

"Or is it bigger stuff?" interrupted Zee, clearly enjoying herself. "Like a TV? Or a bike would be nice**...no, wait,"** she frowned, **"I'm being silly. A cat couldn't move a bike. Its feet wouldn't reach the pedals."**

"I'm not sure a cat could move a TV either," I pointed out, but Aunt Zee was on a roll.

"Oh! What if it's not the cat," she gasped. "It could be **Santa!** Leaving gifts for you and Dave! November **is** a bit early but…"

"It's definitely, definitely NOT SANTA!" snapped Mrs Poshpants crossly.

"Aaaahhh. I see!" nodded Zee, looking sympathetic. "Dave on the naughty list, is he? I did wonder because…"

"Oh," cried Mrs Poshpants pulling a blank, silent phone from her purse. "Oh, I need to take this call. Sorry!"

And with that, the poor woman turned and ran for it.

"Zee!" sighed Aunt Nina, shaking her head. "You **really** shouldn't wind her up like that,"

"I know, but they're both so rude!" Aunt Zee pointed out and then she shrugged. **"Plus it's fun!"**

Aunt Zee grinned and winked. But as we turned back to our own garden, her face fell.

"What on Earth!" she frowned. **"How did that happen?"**

On the wall, down near the street, sat three pumpkins flickering in the dark.

Only three!

Where was the fourth?

CHAPTER THREE

"Oh noooo!" gasped Hannah pointing. "Aunt Nina, look!"

Aunt Nina's pumpkin had fallen off the wall and smashed, like an orange Humpty Dumpty!

"Oh what a shame!" said Nina frowning. "The wind must have blown it off."

I looked around the front garden and then up into the branches of the big conker tree next door. Nothing was moving. No breeze at all. The night was still.

As always, Hannah was the first to think of something kind to say.

"You can share my pumpkin Aunt Nina!" she

said, patting her arm.

"Good idea!" said Aunt Zee. "And let's move the rest to the floor!"

I was about to help when I got a really odd feeling. Like someone was watching us. As I turned, I could have sworn something moved in the window of the shed.

"Aunt Nina?" I asked slowly. "What do you keep in your shed?"

Nina paused, looking up to the top of the drive and the old wooden shed. It filled the space where you'd expect to see a garage. But this thing looked like it was falling to bits.

"Hardly anything in there," shrugged Nina. "Just a few of my old gardening tools..."

"Tools she never uses!" teased Zee, gesturing round the garden. "We never go in there. It's just a hotel for spiders. I wonder if we should **charge** the spiders rent for staying there. Although, do spiders have much money...?"

I grinned, but Hannah just shuddered. (She's not a fan of spiders.)

"Come on!" said Nina, seeing Hannah shudder. "You're getting all cold and shivery. Time to get you two into bed."

★★★

Up in the spare room, Sugar and Blaze were tucked into our beds looking like any old average toys. But the second our aunties said goodnight and headed back downstairs...

Rustle Rustle Rustle

...the toys sprang to life.

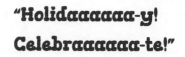

**"Holidaaaaaa-y!
Celebraaaaaa-te!"**

sang Sugar, with a cheerful loop the loop.

"Shhhhhhhh,"

grumbled Blaze. "Mum and Dad will hear."

He blushed suddenly, his blue cheeks turning purple.

"Whoops," he said, remembering. "I meant 'The *aunties* will hear'."

Sugar blasted her sound blocking magic at the door so that we could talk without being heard.

"How could you forget that we're on hoooolidaaaaaaaay?!" sang Sugar happily, **"You're such a ninnnyyyyyy!"**

"I am not!" grumbled Blaze, snuggling under my arm. "Anyway, how's the aunty holiday going?"

"Really good!" said Hannah. "We carved pumpkins."

"And I carved a dragon into mine," I chipped in.

"Really?" Blaze smiled. "I'd love to see that!"

"Maybe you can!" said Hannah, and she slipped out of bed, padding over to the window.

"Look!" she said, pointing down to the wall near the street.

Sugar flew to her shoulder.

"They are suuuu-uuuuu-uuu-uuuuuuu-per!" she sang.

"That one with the zig-zag mouth is mine," said Hannah, "And the dragon one is Jo's and..."

Hannah paused, pressing her forehead to the glass.

"That's odd," she said. "Where's Aunt Zee's?"

Blaze and I joined them at the window.

I peered down to where our pumpkins sat by the wall, as if huddled together in the cold and Hannah was right.

Now there were only two!

Then I saw it again! A shadow **WHIZZING** through the dark, **DARTING** across the grass and gone. A rat? No! Too big. A cat maybe?

"I guess Aunt Zee brought hers back inside," shrugged Hannah.

"Why would she do that?" I asked.

"Not important right now," sang Sugar. **"We need to pick a holiday lullaby-yyy-yyy-yyyyyyyy!"**

"Oh boy!" muttered Blaze. "Here we go again!" He shot back under my covers and covered his ears with his paws.

"It needs to be something about Bonfire Night," she sang thoughtfully.

Hannah grinned as we padded back to bed and Sugar gave a theatrical **"Ha-hem!"**

"Baby I'm a firewooooooooork!"
she began, wiggling her hips.

"I shoot

across

the

sky-y-yyyyyyy"

Sugar **WHIZZED** round the room, lighting up her skin so it turned red, then green, then purple. I had to admit, she did look a lot like a firework which was very fun. Shame about the noise though!

Hannah loves Sugar's singing. She gave a happy sigh as she snuggled down to sleep.

But as Sugar screeched on and on about being a firework, I couldn't sleep. I couldn't stop thinking about Aunt Zee's pumpkin.

Where had it gone?

CHAPTER FOUR

The next morning when we went downstairs for breakfast, the kitchen was in absolute chaos!

"What's going on?" cried Hannah, her eyes wide as we both took in the scene.

Everything, and I mean EVERYTHING, was covered in sloppy brown toffee.

In the middle of the mess stood sensible, reasonable Aunt Nina with a wooden spoon in her hand...and a pan on her head.

"I'M BEING A CHEF!!!" she screamed, a crazy glee in her eyes. "And I'm making toffee apples."

Looking around I could see some toffee apples.

But I could also see some toffee carrots, an oozing pile of toffee books, and even a toffee jumper dripping from the back of a kitchen chair.

"Erm, are you...feeling okay, Aunt Nina?" asked Hannah.

Nina looked between us as if she wasn't quite sure who we were and then...

"I'm a chef!" she repeated, grinning.

"Okaaaay," I said, trying to stay calm so I could think. "And where's Aunt Zee?"

"She went out somewhere," shrugged Nina. "Now go get your trainers!"

That seemed like an awful idea! Everything in the room was drenched in toffee and my trainers were almost new!

"Erm....Why?" I asked, stalling for time.

Aunt Nina winked.

"Just a little **toffee apple treat...for your feet.** Oh, that rhymes... **like a song!**"

And as this idea popped into her head, our normally sensible Aunt Nina held up her wooden spoon like a microphone and started to sing.

"I'm a singer AND a chef! A singing chef!"

Hannah was so alarmed that I thought her eyebrows might shoot off the top of her head.

"Go get the toys!" I hissed. "They'll know what to do. I'll stay here and keep an eye on her!"

Hannah nodded and **DARTED** back upstairs.

Meanwhile, Aunt Nina had started to dance around the room singing:

Try a shoe (it's good for you).

Great to eat, once it's sweet.

Think a cactus is too prickly?

Dipped in toffee - it's just tickly!

Kids aren't picky, if its sticky.

Lovely toffee, scoff scoff scoffy.

"Now that's what I call a sooooong," sang Sugar, flying into the kitchen and wiggling her hips to the beat.

"This is no time for singing, Sugar!" wailed Blaze looking round. "Who did this! Oh, I bet it's a magical baddy again!"

Like I mentioned before, we've had a lot of trouble with magical baddies since we got the toys. Maybe magic attracts more magic or something!

"Check the cupboards!" said Hannah quickly.

But Aunt Nina had other ideas.

"You're a nice talking dragon," she said dreamily, and she pointed at Blaze with her wooden spoon. "Would you like to be dipped in toffee and shoved on a stick?"

She started moving towards him with a weird glint in her eye.

"Erm...well...that's a very kind offer," babbled Blaze, "Maybe...erm....maybe later?"

"Maybe later?" echoed Nina, nodding thoughtfully. **"Okay! Well I suppose I am a bit tired right now."**

"You are?" squeaked Blaze hopefully.

"Oh yes!" she nodded. **"I've been up all night making toffee apples!"**

And just like that she lay down on the sticky table, cuddled up to a toffee coated teapot and began to snore.

"Well I guess that's one less problem," I said. "Now what?"

Sugar and Blaze were whizzing round the kitchen checking each cupboard and drawer in turn.

"No baddies!" said Blaze eventually. "Whatever it was must have gone!"

"We need to find Aunt Zee," said Hannah firmly, *"and check she's okay!"*

"Good plan!" I nodded. "Aunt Nina said she went out so... maybe the front garden?"

But there was no sign of Aunt Zee outside. In fact, the only person in sight was Mrs Poshpants, standing in her own front garden in her pyjamas!

"Morning!" called Hannah with a wave.

Mrs Poshpants looked round in surprise and...

"I'M A SQUIRREL!" she screamed.

"Oh no no no no!" worried Blaze. "Looks like the magical baddy has muddled her up too."

"But who's doing this?" I wondered aloud.

"NUTS!" screamed Mrs Poshpants cheerfully.

"Really?" gasped Sugar. **"Evil NUTS sending people dotty? Sounds about right for an autumn adventure."**

"I don't think that's what she means," said Hannah. "Look!"

Mrs Poshpants had bent over and was now digging with her paws...hands...well, whatever!

The point is, her perfect front garden

was now full of holes.

"Mrs Poshpants, have you been burying **nuts** in your garden?" I gasped.

She turned slightly and for a horrible second I thought she had grown an actual squirrel's tail. But it was just a brown feather duster taped to her trousers.

"NUTS!" she agreed with a nod.

Mrs Poshpants scurried over to the bushes between her garden and ours. Then she held out her posh handbag looking very proud of herself. It was chock full...of chicken nuggets!

"NUTS!" cried a gleeful Mrs Poshpants, and she scooped up a handful of nuggets from her handbag and flung them into the air.

"NUTS. NUTS. NUTS!"

Blaze **WHIZZED** round, snapping the falling nuggets from the sky and gobbling them up.

"Tasty!" he grinned. "For nuts."

"NUTS. NUTS. NUTS!" cried Mrs Poshpants, scattering more chicken nuggets.

"You definitely aaaaaaare nuts," agreed Sugar, nodding.

"Cuck-oo!" added a voice from somewhere nearby.

I looked over to their conker tree and up in the branches in his pyjamas was...

"Mr Poshpants!" I gasped. "What are you doing up there?"

"I..." he said, in a very snooty voice. "...am an owl...Cuck-oo!"

"But you just said 'cuckoo'," Hannah

pointed out. "Owls don't normally say 'cuckoo'."

Mr Poshpants peered down his nose at us.

"I am incredibly smart," he said smugly, **"and the owl is the smartest bird alive so I MUST be an owl."**

But then...

"**Cuck-oo!**" he blurted. "**Cuckoo! Cuckoo!**"

"I'm not sure you ARE an owl, Mr Poshpants," suggested Hannah in her gentlest, kindest voice. *"I think you might be a cuckoo."*

"He's not really a cuckoo or an owl!" giggled Sugar. **"He's just a man up a treeeeeeeee who's gone completely nuuuuuuuts."**

"NUTS!" agreed Mrs Poshpants, flinging more nuggets.

"Argh!" shouted Hannah, as a nugget smacked her on the nose. *"SERIOUSLY! who's doing this? where's the magical baddy?"*

I looked around the two front gardens.

"THERE!" I cried, pointing just as the black thing *SPRANG!*

It burst from its hiding place in the bushes and I saw it at last. The thing I'd almost seen in the dark. The thing that had watched us.

For a second its body made a long dark line, like a smudge on paper. Then it was gone, across the grass, around the corner of the house and out of sight.

"STOP THAT THING!" I yelled, and we *SPED* after it.

CHAPTER FIVE

As we **DASHED** up the drive, I saw the door of the old shed was hanging slightly open.

Hannah snatched up a branch from the edge of the drive and held it high, ready to smash stuff.

Hannah is like a ninja when it comes to being ready for a fight. She could hold a teaspoon and make it look scary.

"Come out!" she shouted at the shed. "I'm armed and dangerous. Come out with your hands up!"

There was a snigger from inside the shed. But then something did prowl lazily back into the dark doorway.

And that something...was a cat.

A sleek, black cat with a swishing tail and a joyful twinkle in its eye.

"I think you mean 'paws up', darling," it drawled in a lazy voice. *"Because as you can see, I don't have any hands!"*

"Just get out here!" growled Hannah.

"But what do you want with ME?" asked the cat. *"I haven't done a thing, darling!"*

"That's not true!" I said. "I've seen you lurking about in the garden!"

"Lurking?" said the cat, pulling a face. *"What an ugly sounding word!"*

"And you ran for it when we spotted you!" said Hannah, pointing her branch accusingly. "That's suspicious!"

"Well then let me explain," said the cat. *"You see, my name is Poopsy and I..."* she paused for effect, *"...am an artist!"*

"Knew it!" sang Sugar gleefully. **"This one's mad like the others. Mad as a jelly rollercoasteeeeer!"**

"Shush, Sugar!" scowled Blaze. "We need to get to the bottom of all this!"

"He's right," agreed Poopsy. *"It IS all about bottoms really. Let me show you!"*

There was a loud

PAAAAAAAAAAAAAAAARP!

and I'm sorry to say that it came from Poopsy's bum!

"Aha!" she cried joyfully. *"Here comes another little work of art. Back in a tick, darlings!"*

She glanced around carefully then **SHOT** across the drive to hide in the nearest flower bed. Then she squatted down and... well you can probably guess what she did.

NO PEEKING – ARTIST POOPING

"Yuck!" cried Blaze, covering his eyes as Poopsy stalked back towards us looking smug.

"Well?" demanded Poopsy. *"What do you think to my ART, darlings?"*

"Erm...a bit gross?" grimaced Blaze, looking more green than blue as he tried not to sick up his nuggets.

"...And stinkyyyyyy!" added Sugar brightly. **"Let's not forget that!"**

"Oh, stop! Stop!" purred Poopsy. *"So kind! You're making me blush, darlings."*

Just then there was a loud

BEEP BEEEP!

and Aunt Zee's car rolled onto the drive.

"Eeeeek! That'll be one of my fans!" gasped Poopsy. *"I can't be discovered near my art. I always work in secret!"*

And with that, Poopsy SCARPERED back into the shadows.

"Aunt Zee!" cried Hannah, running down the drive towards the parked car. "Something's happening. We need you to....oh!"

Hannah had stopped suddenly and as I caught up with her I could see why. Aunt Zee's car was full of pumpkins.

Hundreds of them!

Whoever was doing this had sent her crazy too!

And then Aunt Zee herself came leaping out from the car with a wild gleam in her eye.

"I'm a farmer!" she cried excitedly. "Just been out harvesting pumpkins...from the supermarket! **Now let's get them into the house!"**

Immediately she began pulling pumpkins from the car and trying to make a tower of them in her arms. But as you've probably realised

pumpkins don't exactly stack together!

So every time she picked up one, she lost her grip on another and it bounced away down the drive. Not that she seemed to notice.

"Aunt Zee," tried Hannah, but Aunt Zee wasn't listening.

"Wait!" she cried suddenly. **"I've had an idea!"**

She tucked a pumpkin under each arm, gripped the third between her knees, and began to waddle for the door like a lumpy orange penguin.

And just when it looked like things couldn't get any worse...

"Not a chance!" screamed a voice.

"You're not bringing those in here!"

It was Aunt Nina, awake again and standing

in the doorway, hands on hips.

"Oh yes I am!" yelled Zee and she began to waddle as fast as she could, charging towards the house.

Nina screamed and slammed the door shut, but Zee changed direction. She waddled with all her might towards the open kitchen window.

"In they come!" cried Zee, and she started posting pumpkins through the open window and into the house.

But in a flash Nina was back at the door, flinging the posted pumpkins back down the drive with a joyful, **"Out they go, you stinky old sea-saw!"**

I'm not sure why Aunt Nina thought 'see-saw' was an insult. It's fair to say they'd both totally lost it at this point!

Anyway, Aunt Zee shrieked with fury and started running back to the car to get more pumpkins. But then Nina turned up at the kitchen window with a new plan.

"Take that!" she cried, chucking a toffee carrot at Zee. **"And that! And that!"**

"Yikes!" screamed Zee, as toffee-soaked veg started to rain down all around us. **"Take cover!"**

Blaze whipped past my head with an alarmed expression on his face and a toffee sausage stuck to his wing.

"Next door's garden!" he yelled gesturing madly. "Quick!"

We dived over the bushes, but of course next

door's garden had its own problems.

"Nuts!" screamed an alarmed looking Mrs Poshpants, and she started pelting us with her chicken nuggets.

"Next door's BACK GARDEN!" corrected Hannah and she **SPED OFF** up their drive, away from the chicken missiles.

Panting for breath, we all followed and spilled into next door's back garden, slamming the gate behind us.

"Now what?" wailed Blaze. "Maybe we…"

But before he could finish something REALLY odd happened.

"Shushhh!" hissed Sugar.

Sugar, the noisiest fairy in the world, was telling US to be quiet! The world really had gone mad!

She pressed a finger to her lips in a silent warning and then **ZIPPED** across the garden to peek over the fence.

When she flew back, I could tell from her amber skin that it was MORE bad news. Amber skin meant 'get ready'. It was almost always a very bad sign!

"It's him!" Sugar whispered. **"The one making all this happen. He's in your aunties' back garden . . .**

. . . It's The Baddy!"

CHAPTER SIX

"Come on then," whispered Hannah, snatching up another fallen branch from the ground and tiptoeing towards the fence.

"Always towards the danger," grumbled Blaze under his breath. "Why are we never creeping towards something good...**like an ice cream van?"**

"Shhhh," hissed Hannah. "Listen!"

On the other side of the fence, something had started to speak.

"THE THING IS, DOCTOR, WHO AM I?" said a worried voice. "AM I A SINGER, OR

A **DANCER**, OR A **DECORATION?**"

"PSSSST!" hissed Sugar, waving.

She was beckoning us towards a crack in the fence.

Time for some sneaky peeking!

"AND WHAT IF I WANTED TO BE **SOMETHING MORE?"** the voice went on as we pressed our heads together to peer through the crack.

AND THERE IT WAS...

sitting in the middle of the garden was

a pumpkin...

a very <u>alive</u> pumpkin...

a pumpkin with a huge round mouth!

Hannah tugged at my arm.

"That's Aunt Zee's pumpkin!" she mouthed. "That's NUTZO!"

I nodded. The pumpkin was talking again.

"I HAD AN UNCLE THAT WENT INTO

A **CURRY, YOU KNOW,**" said Nutzo proudly. "MAYBE I **COULD DO THAT?**"

Who was he talking to?

The only thing near him was a shiny conker laying on the grass.

The conker! Oh no! Maybe that was alive too!

The pumpkin gave a deep sigh.

"**THAT'S WHAT** I **LOVE ABOUT YOU DOCTO**R **CONKER,**" said Nutzo. "YOU'RE **SUCH** A **GOOD LIST**ENER."

DOCTOR CONKER! Oh, this was bad!

I held my breath, expecting the conker to spring to life and say something...

...but it didn't. No magic. It was just an ordinary conker.

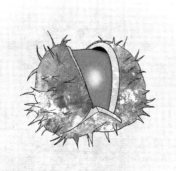

Nutzo gave a deep sigh.

"I **HAD** **DREAMS**, YOU KNOW...BIG **D**REAMS!"

He sniffed and a pumpkin juice tear dribbled from one of his triangle eyes.

"I **WAS GOING TO COMPOS**T **DOWN** **T**O MUSH SOME DAY. YOU KNOW, START A FAMILY!"

The conker didn't say anything...because as I've mentioned, it was just a conker!

"**THIS** IS ALL **HER** FAULT!" Nutzo shouted, turning towards the house, "**WHO** AM I? AM I A SINGER OR A DECORATION?"

His orange body started to tremble like a volcano about to erupt.

"**TIME** FOR **SO**ME ANSWERS!" he screamed and instantly new green shoots burst from the stump of his stalk.

Loads of them!

They grew and grew, faster and faster, slithering down towards the floor like snakes. And once they touched the ground they lifted him up like an ugly, orange spider on strong, green legs.

"YA-HA-HA HA!" he cackled to the sky. "YA-HA-HA HA!"

And then he scurried away up the garden path towards the house!

"After him!" yelled Hannah. "Blaze, burn through the fence."

"Hannah, you can't go burning down people's fences!" I reasoned. "We'll have to go round. Come on!"

I grabbed her arm and that's what we did. We ran back down the Poshpants' drive and through their front garden, dodging flying chicken nuggets as we went!

Then we dived through the bushes, back into our aunties' front garden. No sign of the Aunties and luckily the food fight seemed to have finished.

But the monster pumpkin wasn't there! No one was there! Except...

"Poopsy!" cried Hannah. "There's a pumpkin monster."

"Yes I saw that!" said Poopsy, considering. "Is it art, would you say?"

"Art?" spluttered Blaze.

"Yes, ART!" Poopsy continued thoughtfully. "Because I love a good sculpture as much as the next cat but that thing seemed a tad dangerous, darling!"

"Poopsy! We're in a hurry here!" I cried.

"*Righto!*" said Poopsy. "*That makes sense given the circumstances.*"

"What circumstances?" asked Hannah frowning.

"*Well perhaps I should have told you straight away!*" said Poopsy. "*But you see I was wondering what makes something ART and...*"

"**Poopsy! Out with it!**" yelled Sugar.

"*The pumpkin monster took your owner,*" Poopsy announced. "*That Aunty thing.*"

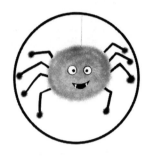

CHAPTER SEVEN

"Which one?" I gasped. "Which aunt did he take?"

"Why?" asked Poopsy in surprise. **"Is one of them more special than the other?"**

Fair point! I didn't fancy explaining to Mum how we'd lost EITHER of our aunties!

Poopsy shrugged.

"It was the one playing with all the pumpkins," she said. **"The sticky toffee one went back inside."**

"Where did the pumpkin monster take her?" snapped Hannah, which I have to admit was a much more useful question than mine.

Poopsy pointed.

"The shed," she said. "And I think I'll tag along with you because..."

I'm guessing her reason was something to do with art and sculpture and things but we never heard it because Hannah ran off. Which left the rest of us (including Poopsy) racing after her.

We blasted into the shed, ready for some kind of fight...but the pumpkin monster wasn't there.

As my eyes got used to the gloom I realised the whole place was covered with silvery spider webs.

And I mean everything!

Every rusty gardening tool and dusty plant pot was attached to the next with hundreds of sparkly threads!

I was just starting to think that Poopsy must have made some kind of mistake sending us into

the shed when a deep voice boomed
out...

"I AM

DARK DANCER...

FANG FIGHTER...

SPIN CYCLER...

...WAIT," said the voice, sounding suddenly
thoughtful. "Does that last one make me
sound a bit like a washing machine?"

"It really does!" sang Sugar. **"I have
some of Blaze's smelly socks to clean
if you're a washing machine
monster?"**

"My socks aren't smelly," grumbled Blaze. "I
don't even wear socks!"

Sugar giggled.

"As I was saying," said the voice, sounding annoyed. "They call me FANG FIGHTER..."

"But where ARE you?" interrupted Hannah, glancing round the gloom. "Are you an INVISIBLE monster?"

"I'm right here!" said the voice, sounding more and more cross. "HERE!"

Hannah shrieked.

A **SPIDER** the size of an apple was dangling just in front of us, wiggling its hairy legs.

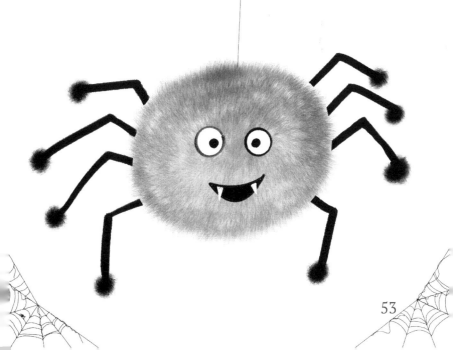

"Wait! You're not a monster!" I laughed. "You're just a spider!"

"Same difference," grumbled Hannah.

Hannah is REALLY not a spider fan!

"But you're so cute," sang Sugar. **"Are you suuuuuuure people call you FANG FIGHTER? I'm not seeing any fa--aangs?"**

"Well..." he paused. "They don't call me Fang Fighter YET. But I'm hoping it might catch on, you know, if I tell enough people."

"Okaaaaay," said Blaze, looking unconvinced.

"We could call you Tummy Tickler," sang Sugar cheekily. **"That's a cute name!"**

The spider's lip wobbled and he looked like he might cry.

This would normally be Hannah's cue to say something kind, but Hannah had her eyes shut.

Like I said - not a spider fan!

"Erm...Why don't you tell us what people call you at the moment?" I suggested.

There was a long pause and then...

"Cedric," admitted the spider. "Cedric Spider. My Mum liked it because of the alliteration."

"But Cedric starts with a 'C' not an 'S'," I pointed out.

Eight hairy legs shrugged.

"But it SOUNDS the same," he explained, "and spiders can't really spell."

"And yet they know all about alliteration," said Poopsy, raising an eyebrow.

"Yes," nodded Cedric, sounding suddenly more cheerful. "That IS a bit odd, isn't it? I guess being smart and being able to spell are very different things."

A quick glance at Hannah revealed she still had her eyes screwed shut. So it looked like it was up to me to get everyone back to the point.

"Cedric, we're looking for a pumpkin monster," I said. "Did you maybe see..."

"Oh I saw him alright!" said Cedric with a shudder. "He looked angry so I hid in my plant pot!"

"And youuuuu want people to call you Fang Fighterrrrrr?" sang Sugar, shaking her head. **"Not gonna haaaaaappen!"**

"Never mind that now!" said Hannah, with her eyes still shut. "Did you see where the pumpkin went, Cedric?"

Cedric nodded and wiggled his legs towards a huge sparkling web in the corner.

"That web is a doorway to another

woooooorld," he said in a **SPOOKY** voice. "The pumpkin went...through theeeeeeere!"

"Then that's where we're going," said Hannah.

She sounded very determined for someone with their eyes shut.

"Are you sure you want to do that?" asked Cedric. "Because I think I heard that old pumpkin screaming from the other side."

Blaze made a little whimpering sound then coughed to cover it up.

To be honest, I understood how he felt. This day was already **QUITE SPOOKY** with a **PUMPKIN MONSTER** and **A SPIDER AS BIG AS A TENNIS BALL.**

I wasn't sure I wanted to add screaming into the mix but...

"He's got our Aunt Zee," I shrugged. "We have to!"

Cedric nodded.

"Okay then. If you'll just solve my riddle, I'll be happy to let you past," he said. "I'm the guardian of the web, you see. Can't just let anyone barge through."

I was about to argue that he'd just let the pumpkin 'barge through', but before I could, Poopsy snorted.

"*Daaaaarling, I'm a cat,*" she laughed. "*Cats go wherever they like.*"

And with that she **SPRANG** into the sparkling web...and disappeared.

Hannah had opened one eye to take a peek at the web.

"*Sorry Cedric,*" she called, without looking in his direction. "*I'm afraid we're in a bit of a hurry!*"

And she too **JUMPED** right into the web and disappeared with Sugar flying after her.

"Well, I'd quite like to do a r-r-riddle," stammered Blaze, eyeing the web nervously. "A really, really LONG riddle."

Both Blaze and Cedric looked at me hopefully but I shook my head. We had to catch that pumpkin monster and rescue Aunt Zee.

"Okay. No riddle," sighed Blaze, his wings sagging. "Let's get this over with."

And ignoring Cedric's protests, we **LEAPT**

through the web...

...and immediately wished we hadn't!

CHAPTER EIGHT

I was trapped.

My body was wrapped tightly in something black and I knew I must be upside down because I could feel the blood rushing to my head.

"Hannah!" I shouted.

No answer!

Somehow, with a frantic, wriggling push I managed to pop my head out of the blackness and what I saw wasn't exactly good news.

I was dangling upside down in a huge tree far, far above the ground.

And somewhere nearby Hannah was screaming.

"Yaaaaaaahooooo! Wheeeeeeeeeeee!"

Wait! That wasn't right! That sounded like her happy 'I'm-on-a-rollercoaster' scream.

At that moment, a black bat came flying through the dark night towards me.

But as the bat got closer I noticed something. It had wide black wings, a tiny furry body and a Hannah-like face!

That's right!

Hannah WAS the bat!

"Hannah, how on earth are you a bat?" I spluttered.

"I think the magical web did it," she called, as she swooped backwards and forwards. "Even Sugar and Blaze are bats. Poopsy too!"

Behind her in the dark sky flitted another bat calling out in an unmistakable voice.

"I can FLYYYYYYY! I shall poop my art across the sky for the whole world to see!

I shall poop my art to the moon and back!"

well that was a disgusting thought!

But I had bigger things to worry about right now. I was still trapped!

"Hannah, you've got to help me!" I cried. "I'm stuck in some kind of black sack."

"No you're not," explained Hannah patiently. "It's just your wings."

"My wings?" I gasped.

"Yes. Your wings. Just imagine you're doing a big stretch," she advised. "You'll see!"

I tried to stretch my hands out to the side like

a scarecrow and immediately the black sack unravelled.

I WAS FREE…but also A BAT!

I took a deep breath and flapped out to join the others under a bright full moon.

I was flying!

"This is mad!" I said, looking round. "It was morning when we ran into the shed and now it's dark. What's going on?"

"We've travelled to a completely different woooooooooooorld," sang a purple bat, which I guessed was Sugar.

Looking around I could see that she was right. The street where my aunties lived was gone. All I could see was a forest.

"Why are you worried about what time it is?" giggled a bat that sounded like Poopsy. "Aren't you more worried that we're all bats?"

That was a good point!

"When we go back to our world, I'm SURE we'll all go back to our normal shapes," said a blue Blaze bat, looking very UNSURE.

"We can worry about that later," said the Hannah bat, flitting over to my side. "Remember why we came here!"

"To poop in the sky!" cried Poopsy bat.

"No! To rescue Aunt Zee," corrected Hannah firmly. "Now come on!"

"Everyone should flyyyyy ABOVE Poopsy," sang Sugar bat. "Unless they want a smelly cat poop haaaaaaat!"

She started to giggle but then suddenly her whole bat body turned an icy blue colour.

"What is that aaaaaaaawful soooooound?" she cried, pulling a face.

At first I couldn't tell what she meant but as we flew on I started to hear it too. We all did!

"HEEEEEEEEEEEEEEEEEEEEEEEELP!"

Hundreds of tiny voices were screeching.

"HELP! HEEEEEEEEEEEEEEEEEEEEEEEEELP!"

"Come on!" sang Sugar. **"Quickly!"**

We followed her towards an odd looking tree covered in long green vines and strange black berries.

"Heeeeeeeeeeeeeelp!" screeched the berries.

That's when I realised!

They weren't berries at all!

Each black blob was the head of a bat. Their bodies were hidden, tied tightly to the tree with masses of green vines.

PUMPKIN VINES!

"Help! Please please!" squeaked an especially tiny black head, tears running down his baby bat face. "My wings are all squishedy and hurty."

"That monster," cried Hannah as we all rushed over and began to pull the bats free.

But that was harder than it sounds because as I might have mentioned WE WERE BATS! Instead of hands, we had these hook-y claw-y things at the edge of our wings!

"What happened here?" demanded Sugar the bat as we all began to slice at the vines with our claws.

"P-p-p-pumpkin!" sobbed the baby bat. "He was screaming 'WHO AM I? WHO AM I?' But we didn't know...he got m-m-mad."

The bat that was Sugar turned red with fury.

"Don't worry," said Hannah gently. "You're safe now."

"Thank you! Thank you!" chorused the bats.

As each one was set free they began flitting

around the tree to get their wings working again (because as any bat will tell you, pins and needles in your wings is a terrible thing).

"Did you see where he went?" I called out to the cloud of bats. "The pumpkin, I mean?"

The baby bat flew over to us and pointed high into the tree where another magical web sparkled brightly in the moonlight.

"Through there," he explained. "He wanted to know who he was, so we told him to go and ask Oak-ee the Wise."

"Thanks!" said Hannah.

"Who's Oak-ee the Wise?" I added, but then I realised Hannah had already flown off towards the web.

We all flitted after her, up to the top of the tree. As we blasted through the next magical web I felt my bat wings melting away. Suddenly, I was falling and I mean falling FAST! A scream started to bubble up in my throat but before it could pop out...

We had landed with a bump, in the branches of a tree. A conker tree!

The good news was, we weren't bats any more! The bad news? Well, now we seemed to be hedgehogs.

Hedgehogs up a tree! And that wasn't actually the worst thing.

Dangling in front of us on a sort of conker-seated rope swing was another furious hedgehog that I didn't recognise.

"YOU THERE!" he screamed, pointing at Blaze the blue hedgehog. "CONKERS OR DEATH?!"

CHAPTER NINE

When Blaze didn't answer, the conker-riding hedgehog screamed at him again.

"CONKERS OR DEATH?!"

Blaze gulped.

"Errrrr...Conkers!" he squeaked. "I choose conkers!"

The hedgehog nodded, satisfied, and pointed to a conker-seated rope swing near us.

"Then we shall battle on conkers..." he said before shouting, "...TO THE DEATH!"

"Wait! What!" cried Blaze. "No! In that case, I pick the other thing!"

"What?" sang Sugar. **"The other thing was DEATH, Blaze. You can't pick death, you silly sausage!"**

"OOOOOH!" wailed Blaze. "Someone else pick!"

Hannah stepped forward.

"Are you Oak-ee the Wise?" she asked.

"Of course not!" snapped the hedgehog crossly. "Oak-ee the Wise is an OWL! He lives through there."

He pointed to yet another magical web over his shoulder that sparkled just out of our reach.

"BUT," he added, "NONE MAY GO PAST!"

"What about pumpkins?" asked Hannah suspiciously. "Did you let a pumpkin go past?"

The hedgehog crossed his arms, looking incredibly grumpy.

"Maybe!" he admitted. "But he cheated!"

"Oh really?" asked Sugar innocently. **"And how exactly did he do that?"**

"Well," said the hedgehog, "First he...wait a minute! Are YOU trying to CHEAT too?"

He immediately forgot Blaze and turned to face Sugar, glaring.

"CONKERS OR DEATH?!" he screamed.

"CONKERS!" decided Hannah suddenly and she scampered over to the other conker-seated rope swing that dangled near our branch.

"Wait for me- eeeeee!" sang Sugar hedgehog, running after her.

"Come on everyone!" I yelled and somehow we all leapt onto the massive conker as Poopsy cried,

"I shall poop my art as we swing!" and Blaze wailed,

"Oh please dooooon't!" and our conker sliced through the air. Faster and faster. Straight for the other hedgehog until...

Our conker thwacked into his! There were so many of us that the poor guy really didn't stand a chance.

His conker seat cracked into bits and he fell to the ground.

But he wasn't hurt. Or even bothered!

"Any chance of a rematch?" he called up hopefully from the leaves below. "Best of three?"

"Sorry," shouted Hannah. "Gotta go!"

We scrambled from the conker and dashed over to the magical web, diving into it.

Immediatetly, I felt my hedgehog prickles melting away!

Did that mean we were turning back into ourselves....fingers crossed!

I tried to actually cross my fingers, or hedgehog claws, or whatever!

But then I realised...

I didn't have any fingers...or claws...I only had feathers!

CHAPTER TEN

Looking around I thought we might be in a hole inside a tree. Which would make sense because thanks to the latest magical web...

...we were now owls!

There was a purple sparkly owl, a bright blue owl and...

"I've got wings again!" screeched a black owl. *"I'm off to poop my art across the sky!"*

Poopsy spread her wings but...

"Wait!" hissed the Hannah owl, pointing.

There was no sign of Aunt Zee or the pumpkin but lurking in the shadows was one more owl. And it was HUGE!

"Are you Oak-ee the Wise?" whispered Hannah.

The owl didn't move but a voice hooted out from the darkness.

"YES! HOW CAN I HELP YOU HOO HOO?"

"We're looking for our Aunt Zee," said Hannah. "And an incredibly naughty pumpkin."

"HE WAS JUST HERE," hooted the voice. "HE WANTED TO KNOW WHOO HOOO HE WAS."

"Did you tell him?" asked Hannah. "Did you know?"

The owl was so still it looked like a statue. Its eyes looked like shiny black pebbles and its copper feathers reminded me of autumn leaves.

"I TOLD HIM THAT A PUMPKIN COULD BE MANY THINGS," continued the voice. **"PUDDING-FILLER,** light-giver, face-puller...."

"Wait a minute!" I cried. "You remind me of...Cedric...is that you?"

"WHOO HOOO HOOO HOO IS CEDRIC?" hooted the voice. "I don't know any Cedric. Unless you mean that spider who lives in the shed. Fang-fighter I think he's called."

"It IS you!" cried Hannah. "Cedric, you come out here, right now!"

There was a long pause and then,

"Oh alright," muttered a grumpy voice.

That's when I realised. The owl feathers didn't just <u>LOOK</u> like autumn leaves. They <u>WERE</u> autumn leaves! The whole thing was just a costume.

The pebble eyes thudded to the floor. The leaves rustled and out came...

Cedric Spider.

I thought Hannah might close her eyes again at the sight of our spidery friend, but it turned out she was way too mad to be scared.

"Cedric Spider," she snapped, sounding a lot

like our Mum. "Why on earth are you pretending to be an owl?"

Cedric shrugged.

"People EXPECT a wise old owl," he explained sadly. "They don't want help from a spider. Even though I'm a great helper!"

"But that's not right!" said Hannah frowning. "People should let you be yourself!"

"Can we hurry this up," said Poopsy owl, fluttering impatiently. "I have some art to poop across the sky, darlings!"

She had a point. Not about the pooping, obviously, but about the hurrying.

"Cedric, I don't care if you're a spider or an owl or a...a rainbow unicorn," I told him. "I'd love your help. Can you help us find Nutzo the pumpkin monster?"

"And do you possibly have a magical gift?" added Blaze looking shy. "Because what we've found on other adventures is that it's easier to defeat a magical monster if you have a magical gift."

"Great idea Blaze!" said Hannah, making the blue owl blush a purple colour.

"I can help!" said Cedric brightly. *"Just a sec!"*

He began to zip around, spinning a web and calling out,

"Blast him through this web and see.

By the end he'll be HAP-PEEE!"

With a flourish Cedric pulled down the finished web. Using his many legs he folded it neatly like a tablecloth before handing it to Blaze.

"Speaking in rhyme now are weeeee?" Sugar pulled a face. **"Is that really necessary?"**

"Is singing all the time really necessary?"

muttered Blaze, and Poopsy sniggered.

Sugar stuck her tongue out.

"And after you've blasted the monster through the web, you can jump through it yourselves and it will take you home," explained Cedric. "Any questions?"

"I have one," said Poopsy. "I really want to take my art to the next level. Any tips?"

"He meant do we have any questions about the plan," grumbled Blaze, but Cedric just smiled.

"Cat," he said slowly. "Have you heard of something called..."

He gave a dramatic pause.

"A TIME CAPSULE?"

Poopsy shook her head.

"It's where you bury things underground for people in the future to find," he explained. "To be a truly great artist, THIS is what you must do!"

Poopsy's owl beak fell open.

"Bury my art?" she asked, shocked. "Are you quite, quite sure darling?"

"Oh absolutely!" nodded Cedric. "Bury it as deep as you can dig!"

"Dig..." murmured Poopsy and she fluttered away looking deep in thought.

"That's brilliant, Cedric!" whispered Hannah. *"If Poopsy buries her art then Mrs Poshpants won't keep stepping in it!"*

"Very clever," I nodded. "I'm impressed!"

"Well they don't call me 'Oak-ee the Wise Old Owl' for nothing," he grinned.

"You're a wise SPIDER, Cedric." said Hannah, wagging her finger. *"You should be yourself."*

"But could you be yourself without the rhyming thing?" added Sugar. **"Because you sound like you're in a bad pantomiiiiiiiiiime."**

"Rhyming is fun," grinned Cedric. *"Look! I'll show you."*

He pointed to another magical web in the corner and put on his WISEST voice.

"The pumpkin jumped through there,

So follow him! It's time..."

"...for me to kiss a bear and always speak in rhyme?" finished Sugar. **"Oh drat! Now he's got me doing it!!"**

Cedric winked at me.

"Told you rhymes are fun!" he grinned. "Now off you go and GOOD LUCK!"

"Bye bye, Fang-Fighter," said Hannah kindly.

The spider looked thoughtful.

"You know what? Call me 'Cedric The Wise Spider!'" he grinned. "I'm hoping if I tell enough people it might catch on."

Hannah beamed her approval and we dived through the new web.

I felt my owl feathers fluttering away. Even better, my hands were back.

Phew!

We'd landed somewhere dark that smelled like straw.

Hannah found my hand in the gloom and gave it a squeeze. It was our secret signal. It meant 'BE READY'.

Together we peeked out from our straw hiding place.

We were behind a stack of hay bales in a huge barn. The big wooden doors hung open and moonlight flooded in but it was a strange, cold sort of light.

And there he was!

"I'M **NOT MANY THINGS!**" snarled Nutzo scuttling through the hay on his vines. **"THE OWL WAS WRONG! I DON'T WANT TO BE MANY THINGS!"**

Aunt Zee was sitting nearby on a bale of straw with a dreamy look on her face.

"I love pumpkins!" she giggled. "They can be decorations and pop stars and..."

"STOP IT!" screamed Nutzo, pointing a

vine at her face. **"THIS IS YOUR LAST CHANCE WOMAN! TELL ME—WHO AM I?"**

But before she could answer, his triangle eyes widened with surprise.

"OH, HOW INTERESTING!" he breathed. **"DOCTOR CONKER INFORMS ME THAT..."**

His pumpkin head began to swivel slowly on its vines and his mouth twisted in to an evil grin as he whispered,

"HELLO CHILDREN!"

CHAPTER ELEVEN

There was no time to gasp, let alone to run!

Nutzo shot out a vine that grabbed Hannah's ankle, lifting her upside down.

"No!" cried Blaze, but he was next.

The vines plucked him out of the air and tangled him in green shoots, as Sugar dive-bombed Nutzo, red with rage.

"Let them go!" she screeched, dodging the vines that were curling up to catch her. **"I'm going to autumn squash you, you smelly-bum, nasty-pants, soup-for-**

brains. . . You…!"

"Sugar!" I yelled, dodging my own vines as I ran to help Hannah. "Dust Blaze with your magic so he can grow big and help!"

"I don't need his help," she snarled. **"I'm going to…"**

"Sugar, please!" screamed Hannah, from somewhere inside a swirling mass of green shoots.

"Fine!" snapped Sugar, and she flew over the vines that were holding Blaze, showering him in magical dust.

At once Blaze started to grow, bursting out of the vines that held him.

"Yes!" shouted Sugar but…

"Nooooooooo!" cried Poopsy, pointing her paw in horror. **"LOOK!"**

The magical dust had touched one of the vines and **it too** was starting to GROW!

"WHAT'S THIS!" gasped Nutzo, his eyes wide in delight.

The vine was now as thick as a snake but that wasn't the worst bit! Sparkling magic was creeping up the vine, closer and closer to Nutzo's pumpkin head until...

There was an explosion of magic and I staggered backwards as Hannah screamed and a new deep voice rumbled all around us.

"MWA HA HA HA!"

Sugar's magical dust had made Nutzo huge! He was easily the size of a double decker bus! So massive in fact that he'd blasted through the roof of the barn.

"MWA HA HA HA HA!" he roared again, tilting back his massive pumpkin face to laugh at the dark sky and the full white moon.

"FINALLY I KNOW WHO I AM!" he shouted in triumph. "I'M A MONSTER!"

In a flash Sugar and Blaze were yanked from the sky by Nutzo's fat green vines. And I was right behind them, scooped up and trapped, all of us dangling next to Hannah in our own plant prisons.

(In case you're wondering, Aunt Zee was still free, but she was sitting on her hay bale grinning and dreamy. Basically, she wasn't going to be any help!)

"I WIN," cried Nutzo. **"IT'S OVER!"**

But it wasn't over just yet!

Down on the floor of the barn, I saw a flash of black.

It was Poopsy!

She was slipping in and out of the shadows, moving towards Nutzo's pumpkin head.

Just when I was sure she'd be spotted, she sprang like a panther...right into Nutzo's big round mouth!

And then she started to speak.

"YOU'RE NOT A MONSTER!" came a spooky voice from deep inside the pumpkin.

Nutzo froze.

"DID...DID YOU HEAR THAT?" he asked in a shaky whisper.

But before we could answer, the spooky voice rang out again.

"TO DISCOVER WHO YOU ARE...YOU MUST SEARCH *deep inside yourseeeeeelf!"* wailed Poopsy and she definitely had his attention now.

Nutzo nodded and screwed up his eyes, thinking.

"AM I...AM I," his eyes popped open in surprise. "AM I A **CAT?** I FEEL LIKE **T**HERE MIGHT BE A **CAT** DEEP INSIDE ME!"

"Er no," said the voice nervously. **"KEEP LOOKING.** *Try a bit to the left, maybe."*

Nutzo screwed up his eyes once more, straining to think. Meanwhile, Poopsy's grinning face reappeared, waving from the window of his dark triangle nose.

Was she giving us a thumbs up too? Hard to say because cats don't really have thumbs.

I knew one thing for sure though. She was climbing!

But before I could work out why, Poopsy gave a loud trumpy – **PAAAAAAAAARP!**

Nutzo frowned.

"IS **THERE POO** DEEP INSIDE ME..." he murmured thoughtfully. "AM I SOME SORT OF TOILET?"

"Ah no. That's just a teensy bit of art!" said Poopsy looking proud.

(One word: YUK!)

She disappeared back into the pumpkin and I held my breath. (Partly because things were getting tense and partly because cat poo really smells!

"WAIT," said Nutzo. "I THINK I'M SENSING SOMETHING."

As he spoke, the top of his head began to open like a trap door!

"KEEP concentrating!" warned Poopsy as she climbed out onto the top of his head and gently lowered the lid back into its place.

"BUT I CAN'T CONCENTRATE WITH ALL THIS LOT WATCHING ME!" complained Nutzo, pointing at us. **"HOLD ON. I'LL JUST CRUSH THEM TO DEATH!"**

Immediately the vines began to squeeze tighter. I could hear the others yelling as they fought for breath but there was nothing I could do to help. I was being crushed.

And then...

"OH, EEE, AH," gasped Nutzo and miraculously he stopped squeezing and...

"HEE HEE HEE HEE!"

I couldn't believe it! He was giggling!

Poopsy was **tickling** Nutzo's vines, just where they sprouted from the top of his head.

And as she **tickled** the monster, he was **wriggling** and **giggling** and the vines holding me were starting to feel looser and looser by the second. Maybe even loose enough to...

Yes!

I pushed out of my vine ropes and half climbed (**three quarters FELL**) down to the floor of the barn.

The others didn't waste any time trying to follow me and soon they were all free too!

"Dust him, Sugar!" said Hannah grimly and Sugar nodded, whizzing into the sky.

Now **you probably won't believe this** but Nutzo didn't actually notice Sugar sprinkling him with magical dust. He didn't even notice when he started to shrink!

Because he was much too busy crying and shaking with laughter!

"**OH STOP!**" he giggled as Poopsy tickled. "**STOP! I'M GOING TO WEEEEE!**"

But Poopsy didn't stop. She just kept on tickling.

"The magical gift!" I remembered and Blaze nodded, pulling Cedric's web out from under his wing.

"Hold it up like a football goal," sang Sugar merrily. **"I have a little ideeeeeeea!"**

Hannah and I **DASHED** over to Blaze and we each pulled at a corner of the web until it was stretched out between us.

That's when I saw Sugar.

She was speeding through the air towards the shrinking, giggling pumpkin.

"Here comes Sugaaaaar!" she said, doing her best impression of a football commentator. **"She's heading for the goal... She sees the ball...She shoots..."**

At the last moment, Poopsy sprang to safety as Sugar swooped down and booted Nutzo with all her might.

The monster soared through the air, still

giggling, his vines streaming out behind him.

"HAA-HA-**HEE**-HEE-EEEE" he laughed as he smashed right into the middle of the magical web...

...and vanished.

"GOAL!" screamed Sugar. **"And the crowd goes wiiiiiiiiiiiiild!"**

She whizzed into a joyful loop the loop, her skin bright yellow with happiness while Hannah cheered and whooped in delight.

But just then a cloud passed in front of the moon and a strange chill filled the air. Sugar's golden yellow glow faded and my own skin prickled with fear.

Nutzo might have gone but something was still wrong.

"Not ALL the crowd enjoyed your little trick," hissed a cold voice from the darkness. "I myself am rather furious."

We all looked around for the owner of the strange, angry voice but there was no one there.

"In fact," the voice continued calmly. "I'm so cross, I'm going to destroy you all,"

And then, from behind another hay bale, came something small, round and shiny.

"Allow me to introduce myself," he said. "I...

...am DOCTOR CONKER."

CHAPTER TWELVE

"You've got to be kidding!" complained Blaze. "TWO BADDIES! Have we actually got time to defeat two baddies?"

"Unlikely!" said Hannah. "When Jo writes up these stories they tend to be quite short and…"

"**I'm not a baddy!**" snapped Dr Conker.

"*You're right there,*" agreed Poopsy. "*You're a nut, darling!*"

"**I'm not your average baddy,**" he insisted, "**because I am an evil genius.**"

"**An evil genius is just a baddy**

with a boring speech," sang Sugar rolling her eyes. **"So I guess, here comes the evil monologue."**

She was right.

"Would you like to know a few INTERESTING AUTUMN FACTS before I destroy you?" sneered Dr Conker and he didn't wait for an answer. **"It was I who pushed Aunt Nina's pumpkin from the wall, I who brought Aunt Zee's pumpkin to life, I who sent the grown-ups mad."**

"Hold on! Those aren't really 'Interesting Autumn Facts'," complained Hannah. "You're just listing the nasty stuff you've done."

"Yeah," I agreed. "An interesting autumn fact would be something like, 'Did you know a conker is actually a horse chestnut'?"

"Oh like in that sooooong," sang Sugar. **"Chestnuuuuuts roasting on an open fiiiiiiire. . ."**

"NO. NO. NO!" shouted Dr Conker. **"Not like in that song! That song is about SWEET chestnuts! I'm a horse chestnut!**

You can't roast **HORSE** chestnuts. They're poisonous!"

"So you can't roast horse chestnuts! Now <u>THAT</u> is an interesting autumn fact!" said Hannah cheekily.

Blaze snorted a giggle and flames exploded from his nose in a massive blast.

And just like that Dr Conker was gone. And in his place was something like a lump of coal.

"Whoops!" gasped Blaze.

"Hmmm," sang Sugar poking the charred remains of Dr Conker with her toe. **"Turns out you CAN roast a horse chestnut!"**

"Oh I really feel quite bad about that," worried Blaze, putting his paws to his face.

"It was an accident," I shrugged. "And he had just said he was going to destroy us!"

"Even still," said Blaze with a guilty grimace. "The poor guy didn't even get chance to do his full evil speech thingy."

Hannah looked around the barn.

"Any more baddies want to confess and be defeated?" she called out. "Nope? Then I really think we should get Aunt Zee home."

CHAPTER THIRTEEN

Cedric's magical web had transported us back to our aunties' garden, safe and sound. But I guess we'd been gone all day because the sun was setting behind the house.

It was Bonfire Night!

All the mess from the pumpkin toffee fight was gone. In fact the only pumpkins left were the ones we'd carved in the kitchen. Aunt Zee's pumpkin wasn't a monster any more. It was back in its place by the wall, lifeless and still.

Poopsy dashed away into the bushes, Sugar and Blaze hid and Aunt Zee started rubbing her eyes as if she'd just woken up from a long dream.

"I think I'll call my pumpkin Mr-Happy-Face McGigglesworth the Third," she said, her eyes twinkling with her normal silliness. **"You know, because of his smile."**

"I love the name," Hannah giggled. "But hasn't your pumpkin got more of a hole than a smile!"

"Noooo!" said Aunt Zee, walking down the drive and lifting her pumpkin to show us. **"It's definitely a smile!"**

Next to me Hannah gave a tiny gasp.

Because sure enough, the too-big mouth had disappeared. Instead the pumpkin had a massive whopper of a grin!

But then...

"Urgh!" cried Aunt Zee suddenly holding the pumpkin at arm's length. "There's **a cat poo** inside him. How on Earth...?"

And muttering something about rubber gloves, she marched off towards the house.

"He's smiling!" gasped Blaze as the toys flew back out of hiding to join us. "It must have been all that tickling."

"I'm just glad he's happy!" I shrugged. "And not a terrifying monster any more...I'm really glad about that last bit!"

Blaze gave a little shudder and nodded.

"He kept asking 'WHO AM I?' " said Hannah thoughtfully, "But I guess whoever you are, it can't hurt to be a bit more cheerful."

"...And BEEEEE not-a-nasty-pants,"

added Sugar, nodding slowly as if she'd just said something very wise.

"Well yeah!" giggled Hannah. "That too!"

"Oh, and look," said Blaze pointing to next door's bonfire pile.

There among the old branches, ready to go up in flames, was an Oak-ee-the-Wise shaped pile of leaves. Cedric's costume!

"It looks like Cedric's decided to be himself!" I grinned.

"It's quite a scary thing, being yourself," said Blaze quietly, "but you should always try!"

"Unless being yourself means being a nasty-pants," added Sugar, keen to hammer home her point.

Hannah grinned.

"I still can't believe it was a SPIDER that helped us fix everything!" she said. "Turns out spiders aren't as bad as I thought!"

"Oh I don't know," sang Sugar. **"That rhyming thing was pretty bad!"**

"Look out!" hissed Blaze and the toys zipped into the bushes to hide as the aunties headed down the drive towards us.

"Well, I've **finally** got the kitchen tidy," sighed Aunt Nina, back to her normal self. **"You know, making toffee apples is a lot messier than you'd think."**

Hannah and I shared a secret grin.

Just then there was a call of

COOO-EEEEE!

from next door.

It was Mr and Mrs Poshpants, both back to normal and not a chicken nugget in sight.

To be honest Mr Poshpants still looked a bit smug but he wasn't up a tree shouting 'cuckoo'...

So that was good enough for me!

"We're lighting our bonfire," said Mr Poshpants, pointing. "Fancy joining us for a marshmallow or two?"

"That sounds lovely!" said Aunt Nina, before Aunt Zee could say anything silly.

"Hop on over then," beamed Mrs Poshpants,

pointing at the lowest bit of the bushes. "But mind your step on the lawn. We seem to have a lot of holes for some reason."

"I bet you've got moles," teased Aunt Zee happily. "**Or Mole Fairies**...They're a real thing you know...."

The aunties helped each other to step over the bushes as Aunt Zee continued to explain about mole fairies.

It looked like our autumn adventure was done and dusted. But before we could hop over the bushes to join the Aunties, there was just one last thing.

"Come along, darlings!" drawled a familiar voice.

"Poopsy," cried Hannah as the cat prowled into view. "The magical stuff has ended but you're still talking. Cats aren't really supposed to talk."

Poopsy gave a little shrug.

"I do what I want, darling," she purred.

"I'm a cat!"

And as her tail swished, three little kittens padded out from the bushes to stand by her side.

"And I dashed to get these guys straight away after what that spider told me."

"Oh yes! " sang Sugar, poking her head out of Hannah's jumper. **"Are you going to start burying your stiiiiiinky poooooo?"**

"She means your art," added Hannah quickly.

110

"No darling," Poopsy shook her head. *"Burying art is utter madness. But his advice did get me thinking about the future. So I'm going to start a little school, darling! To teach the artists of the future."*

She gestured to the three kittens. One of them had put up its paw.

"Excuse me, Miss Poopsy. My owner says to only go plop-plop in the litter tray."

"Then your owner is a nincompoop who wouldn't know great art even if they stepped right into it!" snapped Poopsy. *"Now, repeat after me. I am an artist!"*

"I am an artist!" mewed the three little kittens.

And with a delighted smile, Poopsy led them off towards the flower beds to poop some art.

"Right then," smiled Hannah. "Time for that bonfire."

We jumped the bushes and went to join the grown-ups at the fire. Mr Poshpants handed us marshmallows to toast and Aunt Nina went to get the toffee apples as fireworks began to burst across the sky.

"It's been a crazy day!" I whispered to Hannah.

"But it's going to be a yummy night!" she replied with a wink.

And she was right!

Bonfire Night is the best!

Who would YOU draw riding a conker into battle?

What can a <u>whole</u> conker do that a <u>half</u> conker can't?

Look round!

Quiz: Which character are you?

1. You are colouring an autumn leaves picture when the yellow felt tip pen runs out. Do you:
a) Not care! Art is about poop not pens!
b) Grab 8 new colours, one for each of your legs, and go crazy!
c) Ask the pen who you are...and then crush it to death if it doesn't answer.

2. You go to the park to watch a fireworks display. While you're waiting for it to start, do you:
a) Put glitter in your poop and fling it into the sky to entertain the crowds.
b) Hold a sparkler in each of your 8 legs and try to make yourself look like a Catherine wheel...while reciting poetry.
c) Ask a pile of dead leaves who you are...and then crush it to death if it doesn't answer.

3. Someone gives you a toffee apple. Do you:

a) Leave a lovely bit of art in their garden as a thank you.

b) Try to write a poem about apples, until you realise nothing rhymes with apples. Except snapples, and that's not a real word.

c) Ask the toffee apple who you are...and then crush it to death if it doesn't answer.

4. It's your head teacher's birthday. Do you:

a) Poop a statue of the head teacher to celebrate their special day.

b) Pretend you **are** the head teacher, and make a new school rule that everyone may only speak in rhyme **all day**.

c) Ask the birthday cake who you are... and then EAT it to death if it doesn't answer.

If answered mostly A, you're Poopsy. Mostly B, you're Fang-Fighter AKA Cedric. Mostly C, you're Nutzo.

U	K	R	U	P	S	U	G	A	R	W	B	P	A
E	R	E	D	I	P	S	U	I	E	W	L	I	S
A	E	N	N	K	K	E	T	G	G	S	G	T	S
S	K	M	W	B	P	N	T	S	N	E	C	Q	N
K	P	T	R	A	U	E	R	A	L	H	U	U	R
W	K	D	O	T	M	S	A	U	C	I	T	C	G
I	D	E	A	S	P	G	S	I	R	S	O	E	O
D	B	E	W	H	K	O	R	R	B	N	O	P	H
K	B	T	L	W	I	N	E	O	K	I	D	A	E
O	E	O	B	L	N	L	E	E	S	R	H	A	G
A	Z	T	T	N	L	E	R	H	E	W	S	S	D
U	A	Z	E	W	U	S	A	Q	U	U	G	O	E
A	L	E	O	Q	E	R	H	C	M	O	S	P	H
C	B	B	P	E	U	E	R	S	N	I	E	P	A

CONKER	HEDGEHOG
CAT	SQUIRREL
SUGAR	OWL
NUTS	WEB
BATS	PUMPKIN
SPIDER	BLAZE

Go to www.jennyyork.com for lots more FUN!

Audiobooks

Coming Soon!

Printed in Great Britain
by Amazon

86986163R00071